Strange Beauty of the World
Poems

Also by Bill Preston —

A Sense of Wonder: Reading and Writing through Literature

Strange Beauty
of the World

Poems

Bill Preston

A PEACE CORPS WRITERS BOOK

STRANGE BEAUTY OF THE WORLD: POEMS
A Peace Corps Writers Book — an imprint of Peace Corps
Worldwide

Cover photo: Bill Preston
Cover and book design: Marian Haley Beil

For more information, contact
peacecorpsworldwide@gmail.com.

Peace Corps Writers and the Peace Corps Writers colophon
are trademarks of PeaceCorpsWorldwide.org.

ISBN-13: 978-1-950444-03-8
Library of Congress Control Number:2019909457

First Peace Corps Writers Edition, July 2019

In memory of
William G. Preston
Gary A. Preston
Charlotte W. Preston

CONTENTS

Long Shadows of War

Strange Beauty of the World
Poems

SOMEWHERE IN TIME

And every moment is a new and shocking
Valuation of all we have been.

—T. S. Eliot, "East Coker"

· WAITING FOR THE BIG ONE ·

1955. Leith Walk Elementary. Mrs. Bedford herded our second-
grade class down long corridors to an alleged air raid shelter
on the ground floor so that in the event of nuclear conflict
we would be protected. On cool polished linoleum we sat,
duck-and-cover, butts abutting steel lockers, legs crossed,
bodies bent, hands clasped, fingers laced over heads,
cocooned in collective silence. Knowing and fearing
nothing, I wanted the attack to come —
the big one, the fire *this* time —
fervently wished it
huddled there,
time frozen like
the wristwatch
face found
at Nagasaki.
Drill over,
world still
with us,
our teacher
ushered us
back to class
like sheep to
disillusion of
Dick and
Jane and
long div-
ision.

· GUNS ·

We kids amassed arsenals
triggered by WWII movies
and TV westerns my first
a Davy Crockett flintlock
my grandparents bought me
(with a coonskin cap) at Macy's
when I was six which I took
home to Baltimore:
had gun, would travel.

Later a Colt 45 six-shooter
with revolving bullet chamber
and white plastic handle
with black notches
a holster belted my waist
a string tied to one leg
to ensure a quick draw
like sheriff Matt Dillon
on *Gunsmoke*.

There was the derringer
concealed in my sock,
a curious pump rifle
that spat ping pong balls,
and a Luger that fired
suction-cupped darts
with which I stalked

our pet cat and dog
until said weapons
were confiscated
by my parents,
who never allowed a BB gun
only reluctantly conceding
an air rifle.

Various cap and water pistols
some impounded by teachers
at the elementary school
across the street with a hill
in front where we played
a game called "Neat Falls."
Taking turns, one of us
brandishing imaginary rifle
or machine gun would crouch
at the base and proceed
to pick off the others
as we crested the hill
to see who could look
more spectacular in throes
of death. You might throw
back your torso (arms splayed
at imagined impact)
like the Loyalist soldier
in the Robert Capa photo
or stagger writhing,
hands clutching torn guts,
before rolling down the slope.

It was all good fun,
like TV cartoon characters
no bodies really blown apart,
no one ever died.

At our parents' friend's house
one time my brother Gary
and I wandered into a room
found two pistols coffined
inside a wooden case.
Hefting real guns first time
feeling the weight
shaking our hands
we waved and pointed
them at each other
like dueling cowboys
never pulling the trigger
to find out whether
the pistols were loaded.

· N-1 JACKET ·
for Charles M. Schultz

In our neighborhood
1950s Baltimore
the N-1 was for a time
requisite winter wear.
The N-1 was a WWII
Navy winter deck jacket:
rugged, utilitarian, devoid
of ornament, designed
to protect sailors
from the elements.
You got it
at an Army-Navy store
(mine Sonny's Surplus)
plentiful then and cheap
so you had a good shot
at talking your parents
into buying you one.

They were olive drab
with a grayish faux fur collar,
slash pockets, sturdy zipper,
and buttons up the front.
The collar we turned up
to look cool. A flap
on the collar buttoned

over your throat, but that
implied you felt cold so
we of course never used it.

No one looked better
in an N-1 than
a young Paul Newman,
WWII Navy vet,
photographed wearing
his jacket front open,
collar up, hands jammed
in pockets, jaunty smile,
cigarette jutting, strolling
in Greenwich Village.

One day on our block I saw
a teen sporting Charlie Brown
from the *Peanuts* comics
inked on back of his N-1.
Shortly after I spotted a kid
with a Linus drawing on his.
That sealed the deal: I had
to draw a *Peanuts* character
on my N-1. With practice I drew
a good likeness of Snoopy —
supine on doghouse roof,
round stomach, arched leg,
back paws and nose aiming
skyward, black flap ear yielding

to gravity, collar askew —
beaming like life didn't get better.

Wearing my jacket that winter
was a kind of affirmation;
like the character on its back,
I had struck a pose.

· DUTCH RUB ·

Aunt Carolyn and Uncle Bosley would visit our house
when my brothers and I were growing up. Their daughter,
our age, would join us in play — tearing around the house,
the yard, the street. Whenever we got too wild, Aunt Carolyn,
an actor in a local theater group, intervened, warning us
in a grave tone that if we didn't behave Uncle Boz would
give us the Dutch Rub. Heavy silence ensued, in which
we contemplated ramifications of further misbehavior;
more to the point, the meaning of the unsettling phrase.
We had no clue what the Dutch Rub was, no Internet then
to look things up, everything left to our juvenile imaginings.
One time we dared ask Uncle Boz to explain. He sighed,
grimaced, put his head in his hands. Looking up, he shook
his head and, surveying us in turn, whispered,
Believe me, you don't want to know.

His words had the desired effect, the terrible secret never
revealed. Surely, the Dutch Rub was some dreadfully cruel
and unusual punishment. I pictured myself strapped
on a gurney, a demented Uncle Boz working me over,
kneading my body like pizza dough, until my skin
resembled raw hamburger. What the Dutch had to do
with it remained unclear. What I knew about people
in the Netherlands was that they built dikes, windmills,
grew tulips, liked cheese. I was willing to cut them
some slack. And who wanted to risk getting in Dutch
with the Dutch.

Fast forward to an Internet search: what Uncle Boz had called the Dutch Rub corresponds, roughly speaking, to giving someone a noogie. Noogies! When my son was the age I was back in the day of Boz and the Rub, I would sometimes put him in a headlock while horsing around and give him a noogie. Noogies as punishment, let alone torture, never crossed my mind — or his scalp, as the case may be. Looking back, Uncle Boz was never going to inflict the Dutch Rub, knowing full well our imagination would keep our behavior in check. Had he raised instead the specter of an impending noogie, would that have evoked similar existential dread? I think not. Try saying noogie with a straight face.

· TENNIS SHOES ·

They were the quintessence of cool: tennis shoes, as people
in Baltimore called casual canvas shoes — ten-a-shoes to my
young ears. There were many kinds, but Jack Purcells were
top drawer, top notch, top of the line — the Louvre Museum
and Coliseum of tennis shoes — sported by those in the know.
Hemingway wore them. Ditto James Dean and Kurt Vonnegut.
Celebrity cachet aside, what really mattered then was that
my friends and peers coveted the shoes, deemed de facto cool.
Getting a pair was *de rigueur*, a rite of passage.

Then, as now, cool had its price, and there was the rub:
Jack Purcells cost several times more than other tennis shoes.
All pleas to my parents fell upon deaf ears until I began
earning enough money from chores and odd jobs to chip in
the difference for a pair. Thus shod, my spanking-new,
blinding-white tennis shoes were a calling card, attesting
to inherent coolness. I had arrived.

When our family moved to New Jersey, I was shocked to find
that my classmates did not wear my beloved tennis shoes;
rather, plimsolls — sneakers, as they called them. Suddenly,
my alien tennis shoes branded me an outsider. What I wanted
was to fit in, whatever shifting fickle context of cool.
All too soon, I abandoned my tennis shoes for sneakers.

Like a latter-day prodigal son on a sentimental journey, I recently bought a new pair of Jack Purcells — amazed that they have survived the vicissitudes of fashion and are produced now in a dizzying array of colors, patterns, and materials. I still prefer the original white canvas kind.

Call me old fashioned.

· DR. HILL BREAKS THE NEWS (November 22, 1963) ·

Biology. Tenth grade. In buzz and rattle
of adolescent chatter we straggled to class
from gym, shuffled to our seats, restless teens
looking past last period to end of school day
and the impending long Thanksgiving holiday.
I took my usual seat in front of Martin Levine
at the back of class.

Dr. Hill, our biology teacher, radiated
fierce intelligence and serious purpose
that kept you on your toes, made you want
to up your game. One of two
African-American teachers (both PhDs)
he carried himself with quiet dignity
and grace. Like Malcolm X he wore
no-nonsense black browline glasses
bestowing added solemnity. Eloquent,
with a flair for the dramatic, he would
sometimes quote from *Hamlet*:

This above all: to thine own self be true,
And it must follow, as the night the day,
Thou canst not then be false to any man.

Dr. Hill walked into class. The room went
silent. Shaken, face ashen, he looked lost.
Wandering past his desk, he gazed out

the second-floor window, his typical
ramrod posture slumped, as if he were
bearing the weight of the world.
When he finally spoke, his words
were tentative, as if by uttering them
he was confirming what he did not want
to believe.

*The President has been shot. This is a great
national tragedy.*

He sat down at his desk. We tried to weigh
the meaning of his words. Some students
began to cry. Marty and I exchanged
glances of disbelief.

Class was dismissed. Over intercom, we were
told to report to homeroom.

Time slowed, our steps sluggish,
the halls were like a swamp
we had to slog through.

In homeroom Miss Pfaus was in tears.
We took our seats. She took attendance,
perfunctory an act as it was absurd.

A bell must have rung.

I don't remember going home, probably
on the 14K bus. Maybe I walked.

I don't recall speaking, anyone saying
anything.

What was there to say?

· CROSSING CHARLES ·

Sunday mornings in Baltimore my parents drove my younger
brother Gary and me

to the Methodist church on the corner of Charles Street and
University Parkway,

across from Johns Hopkins. A young boy, I would glance over at
the red brick

and white marble buildings on campus, sometimes a few
students by the dorms

playing tennis or tossing around a lacrosse ball in spring or fall
when the weather

was fine — any thought of college impossibly distant, a lifetime
away.

Instead of going to Sunday school during the church service, I
liked to sneak

down to the basement boiler room — alone, or with a fellow
truant, like Gary —

to visit with Jim. The church custodian, Jim Brown was a
middle-aged

African American. Soft spoken, with a wiry, compact body
coiled like a spring,

Jim was the first black person I ever talked with, our
neighborhood working-class

white. In winter, it was wonderful sitting in that snug room,
furnace going, smell

of oil hanging in the warm, heavy air, like being in a private
kingdom and Jim

as king. Jim would tell stories of how it was growing up. One
time he described how,

after a lightning storm, if you touched a metal lamp pole on the
street, you could get

an electric shock — and not just the person touching the pole, but anyone touching

the person touching it. So, he claimed, there might be two or more people stuck

to each other, shocked by the lamp pole. Jim laughed as he spoke, miming how

people got stuck to the pole and to each other, suddenly a kid again, stirred by the rush of memory.

When I started junior high school and began attending church service, I saw less

of Jim. Two years later, my family moved to New Jersey, where I finished junior

and senior high school. In the fall, after graduating from high school, I was back

in Baltimore, in a doom at the university across the street from our old church.

One morning that winter, walking along the campus side of Charles Street, I saw Jim.

A bitter cold day, he was shoveling snow from the church parking lot. Bundled

in a heavy coat with no hat, hunched over, his breath billowing, working rigorously,

shovel moving massive piles of snow, Jim had aged, his hair gone gray. He presented

a solitary figure, pushing against the stark white frozen landscape.

Jim was there: at the church, on the job, working as he had always done.

I stood across Charles, dumb and cold, stuck there for a long moment as if to the lamppost in Jim's childhood story.

How easy it would have been to cross over and greet him.

I moved on.

I never saw Jim again.

· GET A JOB ·

1968. The summer after
the Summer of Love.
Dr. Martin Luther King, Jr.
and Robert F. Kennedy
assassinated two months apart.
The country slouching
toward Chicago
and Days of Rage.

Cleveland in June. My family
had recently moved to Ohio
from New Jersey. Home
from college sophomore year,
stranger in a strange new city,
job prospects slim. My Dad,
whose company sold
industrial chemicals, sent me
down to Republic Steel,
one of his customers,
to speak to a manager.

Entering the office, I walked
past a group of black kids my age
seated on benches, applying
for summer work. I completed
an application, gave it
to my Dad's contact,

and in short order walked
away with a two-month job
in the cold mill.

On the way out, I passed
the black youth, still sitting,
eyes trailing me out the door
as I crossed the level parking lot
and drove back to our house
in the white suburbs.

· OF RICE AND MANGOES ·

April, kindest month,
sweet ripe mango season
in Thailand. Sweet and
succulent, these mangoes
collaborate to create
an exquisite dessert,
khao niaw ma-muang:
sweet ripe mango slices
nestled on warm bed
of glutinous rice
laced with coconut cream
studded with sesame seeds,
and touch of sugar and salt.

Their ephemeral nature
enriches the allure:
sweet ripe mangoes
in season roughly
two months — April
and May to feast, then
ten months famine;
such transience apt,
the Buddha having taught
that all is impermanent.
To those inclined
to self-indulgence,

the slim window offers
sage middle way
between excess
and asceticism.

Partaking is transforming
(and habit forming),
sticky rice and mangoes
at once the holy grail
of sweets, the last word
in treats.

The quest endures:
the perfect plate,
elusive, waits
in restaurant, cart,
or stall,
down side street,
back alley,
night market,
or strip mall.

A compass within
navigates this domain;
there is no map,
only terrain.

· IN THE BAG ·

The gaunt old man that I took
for a farmer, face weathered,
worn like old leather, was eating
at a table across from mine
at a food stall late one evening
in Phitsanuloke.

When our eyes met, he waved
me over. Approaching the table,
I saw a large burlap sack slumped
at his feet. Pointing to it, he nodded
an invitation to inspect.

As I bent forward to look, he opened
the sack, revealing a writhing pack
of monitor lizards: *hia!* considered
a curse by Thais, allegedly unlucky
if you crossed paths in the forest.
When startled, I jumped back, the man
burst into cackling gales of laughter.

Well, this wasn't a forest, I harbored
no ill will toward lizards, curses be
damned. I returned to my table,
finished eating, and then walked back
to my house by the high school,
considering how, without any effort,
I had made someone's day.

· AT FIRST LIGHT ·

Waking before dawn in a tiny hut
on the slope of Mount Bromo,
we bundle ourselves in blankets,
huddle in the cold. Our guide arrives
with mules to summit the crater
at sunrise. Recently married,
young and over the moon,
we might well be on the moon —
a blasted volcanic landscape
everywhere. With saddles rocking,
our mules plod the gritty trail,
world silent, save for rasp and crackle
of hooves on gravel. Reaching summit,
rays of first light play on my wife's hair
and eyes. Her mouth and nose glow
in departing dark, a picture clear
and true as a Vermeer.

· MUSIC OF VACANT CLASSROOMS ·

The second-grade classroom deserted, you stand in the doorway
the day after your son's last day of school. Pint-sized chairs
stacked on pocket-sized tables bristle like porcupines. Books,
paper, and other paraphernalia hibernate on shelves, in closets,
drawers, and cabinets.

Linger a moment, survey the windows and walls bearing
posters, charts, and art, emblems of school year past.

Lean on memory's door, porous and ajar. Step through,
slip in time . . .

Dick and Jane *readers line the shelves,*
Mrs. Bedford's desk stacked with My Weekly Readers.
The Blasting Caps Can Kill! *poster hangs like a threat*
on the wall, subverted by a rogue classmate,
who crossed out Caps, *replacing it with* Farts.
Look closer: your school supplies there
in the cigar box redolent of tobacco, tucked
in your clunky wooden desk.

Step back through the portal, where time present/time past
intersect . . .

Smell the astringent waxed linoleum.
Observe the gangly window pole parked awkwardly
in the corner like a child who misbehaved; present now,
as before.

No need to shut the door as you go,
it closes by itself.

· SLEIGH RIDE TOGETHER ·

Twin ropes looped
in gloved fists
leaning hard
into oblique light
sharp shadows
December afternoon
I crunch and tow
through crusty snow
arms and legs thrusting
breath billowing
like white sheets
in frosty air.

Son astride sled bona fide
(venerable *Flexible Flyer*)
daughter a low rider
in wannabe toboggan
(pink plastic tub)
their laughter overlapping
as I whip right arm forward
slinging his sled ahead
and then my left flinging
her dubious vessel past his
in alternating rhythm
legs feeling the burn
of slow-slog ascent.

At length our reward:
facing down the slope
anticipating the long slide
gravity taking its course.
Ditching suspect toboggan
we pile single file
onto sled
straight and snug
as ellipses.

Pushing off . . .
Flyer sailing
runners hissing
speed-risk ratio just right
laughing our way
to the bottom.

Ride over
I hop off
retake reins
kids aboard
already making
our way back
to the top.

· LAST RECESS ·

We look at the world once, in childhood.
The rest is memory.
—Louise Glück, "Nostos"

Tomorrow is last recess, our daughter informs;
meaning that after graduating from elementary school,
she is moving on to middle school, where there is
no recess.

I ponder the implications, my last recess lost
in distant recesses of memory, where last
recesses repose.

Once the boy I was, in a schoolyard field
beyond blacktop boundary, not hearing
(or choosing not to hear) end-of-recess bell,
staying on, after my classmates returned
to class, playing in grass and dirt.

And consider how leaving elementary school
is much like leaving childhood — not (perhaps)
in one fell swoop, yet certainly a serious swoop,
having much to do with last recess.

All aboard! Last call to play in safe haven
of games, linger on swings, slides, jungle gyms,
walk fences, climb trees, collect and empower
eclectic objects, inhabit private worlds
with friends real or imagined.

This is your life; the limits . . . your imagination.
Whatever you can dream, can be.
"Olly olly oxen free."

· FRIDAY MORNING IN CUSCO CATHEDRAL ·

Faith is, at one and the same time, absolutely necessary and altogether impossible.

—Stanislaw Lem, *The Star Diaries*

Melodious organ music draws you in,
drifts through the dank sacred space.
A mighty fortress: these rocks of ages
fashioned by Inca slaves on ground where,
before conquistadors, an Inca palace stood.

In the sanctuary, a priest conducts the Eucharist;
you refrain, having failed as yet to find the grail,
temptations of faith — ritual, grace, redemption . . .
remain a leap too far.

The music rises, falls, an invisible net cast
to gather the fold: the lost, the found,
the doubting.

Slipping the seductive swell, you surface
on Plaza de Armas, emerging
from turbulent sea, drowning
in light.

· OUT OF ORDER ·

This morning a handwritten sign is posted
on the side door at work:
This door does not work.

It's the door near my cubicle, the one I use
when I want to use the bathroom down the hall.
No problem, I'll use the other door by the kitchen.
That still works. It's further away, but I can use
the exercise, I sit all day.

There are times when I feel like taping a sign
to my forehead:
This person does not work.

The thing is, someone will come later and fix
the door that does not work. But what to do
those times when, at work, I do not work.

Today, I'm lucky: a poem just knocked
on the door that does not work,
and I open it and say,
Come on in.

· COOL HAND PAUL ·

You're a good ol' boy, Luke. You take care. You hear?
—George Kennedy, as Dragline, in the film *Cool Hand Luke*

At work Monday morning, scanning coffee options,
among them *Newman's Own Special Bold* and
Newman's Special Decaf (Fair Trade Certified/
Certified Organic), reminded me you are gone.

Heard first on National Public Radio (which you support)
Saturday night, driving our daughter home from a friend's.
She asked if you were the guy on the lemonade cartons.
(We like your organic lemonade and the funny blurbs on all
your products — bet you had a hand in writing those.)

Again on Sunday morning news shows: Chris Matthews
closed with a brief remembrance, saying how you'd told
one of your daughters this week it had been a privilege
to be here.

And your face on the front pages of Sunday papers
at Stop & Shop late afternoon, shopping for *Gatorade*
and yogurt.

No surprise then to see your picture again this morning
on k-cups with daughter Nell, looking like the couple
from *American Gothic* (knock on Grant Wood); rather,
that the news hadn't sunk in, maybe I couldn't grasp
how nothing could be a pretty cool hand this time.

I choose the *Special Bold*. Even if, on a bet, say, you were going to drink 60 cups of coffee in one hour, this was not the time for decaf.

· WINGTIPS ·

I offered to buy my daughter
a pair of two-tone wingtips
we saw in a Singapore boutique
during the holidays.
How debonair: navy blue
and tan, they were — whirling
perforations dancing
around the sides,
over the toes,
so stylish
and sophisticated there,
on display,
just waiting
to adorn a fortunate
young woman's feet!

She didn't like them, not
her style.

I was certain that, were she to don
the wonderful wingtips, everyone,
everywhere would stop in their tracks
and gasp, *Great shoes!* No matter that
the shoes were on sale (still not cheap),
I could not entice her. Gladly would I
have sprung for those wingtips

(she didn't need them), so much would I
have loved to see her wearing them.

It was not to be.

No point forcing things. Making anyone
(especially the young) wear anything
(especially shoes) not their style
is destined to end badly.

When I was growing up, my parents bought
me a pair of black-and-white saddle shoes.
I loathed those shoes. Saddles may have
been stylish in my parents' day, but no one
in my neighborhood wore them. Bent
on sabotage, with no regret, I scuffed
the saddles to an early demise.

Perhaps my daughter held the spurned wingtips
in similar contempt.

Nonetheless, she would have looked so good
in those shoes.

Exactly what my parents must have thought
about my saddle shoes.

· SHOOTING AN EGRET ·

One sticky Singapore morning,
I'm stalking a nodding cluster
of egrets, their stick legs bending,
rapier beaks poking a grassy field
flanked by splendid banyan trees.
I circle them slowly, space closing,
reckoning that when the striking birds
take flight, I will capture a moment
of grace. Spooked, the birds scatter
skyward. I stand ham-handed, my camera
a useless appendage, and watch
as one stunning bird swerves
and zips over the field,
across an adjacent road
headlong into a passing taxi,
its broken body thudding off
the car door like a muffled shot.

· AS I WAS WALKING ·

As I was walking
in the woods late
one winter afternoon,
at the trail edge, where
it forked, a doe appeared,
peering through spare trees.
Caught in the headlights
of each other's eyes,
we froze. I felt
my mother present —
not as she was at the end,
in rehab, worn down
by age, infirmity,
ready to let go; rather,
my mother who took me
to Enoch Pratt Library
off York Road, where
we would chose books
by Dr. Seuss
and stories
about Madeleine,
Babar,
Curious George,
a Happy Lion,
Ping the errant duck,
which we would read
together at bedtime,

opening doors of wonder
and possibility;
my mother who said,
"Don't compare yourself
to others." The doe
lingered a moment,
turned,
and then slipped
silent
into the forest.

· ELECTION NIGHT 2016 ·

El sueño de la razon produce monstrous.
— Francisco de Goya, from *Los Caprichos*

Watching PBS
late night into
following day
votes amassing
evidence building
outcome emerging
on press
and pundit faces
disquiet first
and then alarm
façades of hope
crumbling
clinging
to reason itself
as it failed
failing
to find a good face
to put on
or some silver lining
feeling pall
falling
on final act

no one wanted
to believe
flailing finally
in vain
to fend off gaggles
of Goya's monsters gathering
their eyes pitiless
pricked ears jutting
batwings batting
dead air

LONG SHADOWS OF WAR

· TRESPASS ·

Visiting a teacher at Ban Vinai camp,
I saw a young Lao woman bathing.
Standing in the open, wrapped
in a *phaasin*, she was using
a plastic bowl to splash herself
with water from a naked spigot.
Our eyes met; we looked
away. She continued bathing,
the surrounding ground closing,
constricting like a python
as I walked on.

· A FITTING GESTURE ·

We were screening refugees
at the Lao camp in Nong Khai,
start of the long vetting process
to resettle families who had fled Laos
after the Pathet Lao seized power,
following years of secret bombing
when the U.S. dropped more bombs
on Laos (though never at war) than
on Germany and Japan in WWII,
the country strewn to this day
with unexploded ordnance.

Approaching a co-worker's table,
a young, one-armed Lao man raised
his hand to *wai* — the prayer-like gesture
of respect made by pressing palms together,
as is the custom in Southeast Asia.

The sight of one hand *waiing* gave me pause,
my two hands busy pressing pen to paper,
filling forms as my translator and I
interviewed another Lao family.

Over lunch break, my colleague said
that the man's arm had been blown off
by a grenade.

The sound of one hand clapping.

· Q & A ·

What is your name?
The Khmer Rouge called us mit. *Comrade.*

Where are you from?
Siem Reap. Near ancient Angkor.

When were you born?
I do not know. Long ago . . . before Year Zero.

How many people are in your family?
There were many . . . before the revolution.

Where is your family now?
Dead.

You have no family members in Cambodia?
Dead.

Your wife?
Dead.

Children?
Dead.

Brothers? Sisters?
Dead.

You are alone here in Phanat Nikhom?
As you see.

How can this be?
Ask the dead.

· HELPING HAND ·

Walking to breakfast
one morning, I spied
a winged insect flailing
on the surface
of a large plastic jar
filled with water
used for bathing
in Galang camp.
With a brush
of my hand, I flicked
the insect free. Landing
in weeds, it was
promptly devoured
by a frog.

· MYSTERIES ·
for Bernie Zubrowski

He went like he came, in curious circumstances: arriving
in Galang one day from Boston Children's Museum, via
India, the Philippines, and Singapore, head full of hands-on
ideas for training teachers; departing months later, on his way
to Istanbul and Paris. Among his many gifts were wondrous
workshops, where he taught us to discover mysteries
in places we had not imagined they might be. Equipped
with drinking straws, we lost ourselves in sensuous pools
and jewels of colored ink — our patterns exploding in bursts
on tissue paper. From designs hand-drawn on spinning tops,
we witnessed twirling tints and shifting shapes configure
kaleidoscopic mysteries we all are. He led us to explore
other realms of the senses: conjuring colossal soap bubbles —
shimmering, quivering, all but alive; orchestrating,
in tropical heat, an ice-cream workshop we could eat.
Trainer extraordinaire, latter-day Prospero, for him it was
all a question of messing about: to see infinity in the arc
of a bubble, eternity in a scoop of ice cream. Bernie said
once that he wanted to leave Galang in a giant bubble,
a suitable swan song. You could picture him, project fulfilled
(which was to please), floating off on the South China Sea,
flowing beard and long hair waving
farewell.

· THE SPIDER ·

One time in Galang I was taking a shower —
encountered a spider . . . not my finest hour.

Its long spindly legs latched onto my toes:
I froze.

While never one prone to claustrophobia,
own up I do to arachnophobia.

I waved my foot wildly right from the get-go;
the spider, tenacious, just would not let go.

Five or six kicks afterwards I nearly took a fall.
At last the spider lost its grip, crashed into the wall.

That was all. That was that.
I left the stall without my hat.

The spider's legs were smooth, not hairy;
even so, it was kind of scary.

· CAMBODIAN MUSICIANS AND DANCERS PERFORM ON CHRISTMAS NIGHT ·

Cambodian music floods the room
like waters of the Tonle Sap, rushing
over parched earth in rainy season.
Tonight, Christmas in Galang,
at a makeshift church in a refugee camp
on an island speck in the middle
of somewhere, it is rainy season.
Rain, in vain, strains to drown
sounds of men plucking, strumming
singing stringed instruments, tapping
vibrant pulse of drums. The musicians,
as detached from the rattling rain
as from mechanics of fingers striking,
stroking, teasing out music, *are* the music.
Their art flows naturally like breathing:
weaving, wrapping the rapping rain
in ancient song.

Dancers appear in classical regalia,
a vision of *apsaras*: celestial spirits
of clouds and water, sculpted in stone,
motion frozen in friezes on walls
at ancient Angkor. Freed from stone,
the women sway, bodies braving lives
lost to killing fields, eyes sweeping
the assembled as if surveying the ruins

of lost kingdoms, smiles enigmatic
as the stone faces of Lokesvara,
bodhisattva of compassion,
at the Bayon.

Rain pounds down on the barracks
and empty classrooms; low-slung clouds
shroud the moon and stars. The world turns
in darkness and in light. More resilient
than bamboo, destroyed but undefeated,
Cambodian musicians and dancers play,
sway on.

· TAKING LEAVE ·

A harbor offers shelter from storms
at sea; in Galang, from storms of life —
temporary sanctuary, relief for seekers
of safe haven. Refugees gathered here,
having fled homelands in Vietnam
and Cambodia, detained for months
or years in a cramped island camp,
today are in transit once more;
this harbor, once an entry point, now
a point of departure, another exit to entries
elsewhere. Lumber scraps stacked near banks
of mud and mangrove reveal no clear design;
rough planks bleaching in tropic sun are not
signposts to particular destinations, point
instead in all directions. Departing families
board squat boats bobbing on green sea;
they shoulder bundles, belongings, possessions
of dispossessed carpenters, nightclub singers,
teachers, soldiers, would-be Americans,
Australians, Canadians — all on their way
to becoming. Amid final hubbub some wave,
some weep; one by one, boats, like bread,
now cast upon the water.

· METAMORPHOSIS ·

To keep you is no benefit; to destroy you is no loss.
—Khmer Rouge slogan

Once there was a high school in Phnom Penh
named Tuol Svay Prey. Commandeered by the Khmer Rouge
in Year Zero, it became a secret prison, Tuol Sleng,
code-named "S-21," where from 1975 to 1979 at least
13,000 people — exact number unknown — were tortured
to death or sent to killing fields.

Everyone brought to Tuol Sleng prison was photographed.
The photos were methodically posed and lighted —
in another world, the photographer might have used his skill for
yearbook pictures. The people look stunned,
confused. The photographs bear no names, only numbers.

After the Vietnamese invaded Cambodia, ousting
the Khmer Rouge, more than 6,000 photos were found
at the abandoned Tuol Sleng prison, others lost or destroyed.
Today it is the Tuol Sleng Museum of Genocide.

Hundreds of photos hang in rows on the museum walls,
thousands of pairs of eyes interrogate the visitor,
all of the people dead, save for a small number
of survivors (exact number unknown).

Of those, one survived because the Khmer Rouge wanted
an artist to paint portraits of their leader, Pol Pot.

Another survived because he could fix sewing machines.

Still another doesn't know why she survived.

The bones of victims still lie unburied. In Cambodia, people
often use the words justice and revenge interchangeably.

During the reign of terror it was said, *The Angkar has more eyes
than a pineapple.*

Decades later, some in power said, *Let bygones be bygones,
dig a hole and bury the past.*

The Tonle Sap reverses its flow with the change of season.
The waters are never fresh, the past does not remain
in the past.

These people who died, they wanted to live —
like you.

· TO DESTROY EVIL ·

As the tires and kindling burned away, Pol Pot's blackened skeleton remained within the orange flames, its right arm and fist raised upward.
—Seth Mydans, *The New York Times*, April 19, 1998

Do not pause the fighting to honor the moment; rather, let sporadic artillery and mortar fire punctuate the proceedings.

With hatchet and hammer fashion a crude wooden coffin.

Place the deceased gently inside.

Add in his straw fan, scarf, belt, and small black knapsack of clothes.

On a base of eight tires craft a makeshift pyre.

Spread the mattress from the deceased's deathbed
over the pyre.

Place the coffin on the mattress.

Set his wicker chair upside down atop the coffin.

Add more tires, stacks of kindling, and drizzle with available debris.

Sprinkle sprays of white and pink fuchsia to garnish the pyre.

At precisely 9:52 in the morning, touch a cigarette lighter (red plastic, disposable) to the stack of kindling.

In Cambodian tradition, give the deceased's bones to his wife and daughter.

Send couriers to scatter the ashes in three places:
> the Tonle Sap, near ancient Angkor Wat;
> Kompong Thom, his birthplace in the eastern jungle, where his revolution was born;
> the western Dângrêk Mountains, where his life and revolution went up in smoke.

Where does the fire go
after the flames burn out?

· THE MUSEUM OF WAR IS KIND ·

*Ho Chi Minh City's War Remnants Museum is an exploration
of the horrors of the Vietnam War from the perspective of the
communist government. As such, the museum is basically a hall
of American horrors.*
—from *HuffPost,* "Travel," April 29, 2014

It's there, on the path beaten by those who come to witness
lose ends of war — relics and wreckage, without and within.
All are welcome: tourists, pilgrims, patriots, penitents, deniers,
the ambivalent. Price of admission: your hearts, your minds.
To miss the exhibits would be a crime.
Hindsight is 20/20
at the Museum of War is Kind.

The guillotine demands your undivided attention,
a no-frills French colonial affair, fully functional,
if rather worn for wear. The gleam is off the blade,
freckled with rust-like flecks of dried blood. Knife
poised above the empty basket implores you to recline.
An open invitation to a beheading
at the Museum of War is Kind.

Behold, our beautiful weapons so meticulously placed,
encased in glass like swarms of mutant insects home to roost:
M16s, grenades, rocket launchers, Claymore mines, napalm,
Agent Orange. Regard the jars of floating fetuses —
a corpus of effects and birth defects, the wonders
of modern chemistry. Seek and you shall find.
Call them collateral damage
at the Museum of War is Kind.

Reflect on photographs framing fear,
decisive moments of life and death, shot
by photojournalists who never got out of war alive:
Burrows Capa Chapelle Huet Potter Shimamoto . . .
Fragments shored against their ruins, images left behind
in the Requiem Exhibition upstairs
at the Museum of War is Kind.

· GRAVES ·

Following mass on the morning of my aunt's funeral,
our small family group traveled to the cemetery,
assembling graveside, a searing hot day in LA.

Near the coffin poised above the open grave, my cousin Tom
and I, born a year apart, found ourselves positioned
opposite a pair of gravestones, silently reading the names
of two young Latino brothers who had been killed within a year
of each other in Vietnam, three decades past.

Standing in sun and silence, I thought about my cousin,
dying of cancer caused by exposure to Agent Orange
during his mid-1960s Army deployment to Vietnam.

I thought about how I had opposed the War, had marched
in Washington, D.C., sat in at the Baltimore draft board,
been called up by the Army in 1970, via lottery, obtained
a deferment, not gone to war.

I thought about the draft years; how, if you had had access
to information and resources, you could have opted out
of military service.

I thought about the brothers under the gravestones, and what
Tom might be thinking.

We did not speak, silence speaking for us,
for the brothers resting beneath the earth,
for our aunt soon to join them,
as the priest spoke some last words.

· SAFFRON ·

Two Buddhist monks
are walking
in Greenwich Village
today, forty years
after RFK was shot,
their saffron robes blazing
in gray June morning
like fire.

busy Saigon street
Buddhist monk
lotus position
self-immolating
fire consuming
saffron robe
flaming aura
body
toppling

The monks pause
at the corner
of Bleecker Street and
Avenue of the Americas.
They look around,
as if standing on the edge
of an ocean, about to test
the traffic tide surging

in this city
of ceaseless motion.

Cautiously, they cross
the Avenue; behind them,
a fountain spouting water
in Father Demo Square.

· VIGIL ·

after the U.S. invasion of Iraq, 2003

Stand together, wands of white,
candles burning in the night;
sending rays of hope with peers,
opposing those who conjure fear.
People gathered in this park,
dwell in light, curse not the dark.
Candles flicker, burning bright,
each a link in a chain of light.
Above, a tree about to flower,
affirming life in ominous hour.

· IN MEMORIAM ·

My goal is to strip things down so that you need just the right amount of words or shape to convey what you need to convey.

—Maya Lin, designer of the Vietnam Veterans Memorial

Wake
at dawn.
Walk
in morning drizzle.
Approach
The Wall:
the granite panels,
the great divide.

Black mirrors rise,
call all to account
for their reflection;
the chiseled roll call
of the fallen,
your name
among the missing.

Witness the ledger
of the lost.
Comprehend
the cost —
you, the living,
aligned
with the dead.

· SONG ·

Bridging two centuries
a whit of dash separates
ninety-four years
(1923 – 2017)
your birth
your death
your story.

Straight out of Jamaica High
(Queens Village, NYC)
you enlisted Army Air Corps
World War II radio operator
flying wild blue yonder
in the Pacific theater
never said much about
what you saw and did
over there. About ten
I discovered
the bayonet
Japanese prayer flag
short snorter
b&w photos
present in your dresser
absent other context
not knowing what to ask.

First born sharing your name
I reported to planet Earth
(Englewood, NJ) moving
to Baltimore early 1950s
growing up
red brick row house
on Glennor Road
elementary school
across the street
sounds of bebop
doo wop early days
of rock 'n roll.

Starting your career
in sales your office
in the Mathieson Building
the city's tallest then
looking up from Light Street
I recall the Art Deco edifice
soaring like a rocket
into boundless urban sky.

You were a Colts fan then
when the team played
in Baltimore same players
played season after season.
You got pumped up
fall Sundays watching

John Unitas
Ray Berry
Alan "The Horse" Ameche
Gino Marchetti
Lenny Moore
"Big Daddy" Lipscomb . . .
play at Memorial Stadium
ecstatic when the Colts beat
the NY Giants back-to-back
NFL championships '58 & '59.
(An old b&w photo shows
brother Gary and me sporting
crew cuts and celebratory
Colts pajamas.) I collected
football cards wrapped
with stiff slabs of pink gum
from the local drugstore
a nickel a pop. When you
tossed me (as Ray Berry)
touchdown passes I imagine
you imagined yourself
Johnny U, didn't you?

When we played Whiffle Ball
in our narrow backyard
chain-link fence three sides
I remember the time
(as Brooks Robinson) I whacked

the whistling plastic ball
straight up over your head
we watched it flutter —
hanging
long beautiful seconds —
arcing
over the crabapple tree
and rear fence
into the alley beyond
my one-and-only
would-be homerun
and the would-be crowd
went wild.

Our family moved back
to Garden State summer of '62
your office on 5th Avenue
near Central Park. Taking
me out to the ball game
watching
Yogi Berra
Roger Maris
Mickey Mantle
Moose Skowron
Whitey Ford
Elston Howard . . .
play in the House
that Ruth Built

entering stadium first time
jaw dropping catching
my breath at first glimpse
of great greensward
spilling to infinity
going . . . going . . . gone.

And times in the Garden
watching
Clyde Frasier
Dave DeBusschere
Willis Reed
Phil Jackson
"Dollar Bill" Bradley . . .
run the court
crash the boards
in thunderous din
and high-top sneakers
players didn't hang on rims
no three-point shots.

Moved the family once again
to Cleveland then we came.
We rode a toboggan that winter
brothers three: Gary Keith and I
piled aboard in line with Mom
you tucked in back securing
us as holding on we sailed
through wind and snow.

When you taught me
to drive a stick shift
the summer I worked
at Republic Steel downtown
trying to master the clutch
I nearly bucked you
though the windshield.

The Vietnam War
dividing us
as the nation.
Having served then
you could not fathom
why I would not now.
Honoring your wish to look
into R.O.T.C. freshman year
walking into the building
seeing men in uniform
doing an about face
knowing in my gut that
this was not the way
I wanted to serve.

Spring of '70 on the heels
of Kent State receiving
a low number in Nixon's
draft lottery I was called up
for an Army physical
at Fort Holabird in limbo

waiting for a deferment
to do community service
in a volunteer program
as a back up I filed
as a conscientious objector
considered moving to Canada.
Clearly confounded but ever
pragmatic you found a counselor
to weigh options relieved when
I got a deferment and worked
as a community organizer
accepting my chosen path
if you didn't agree
our relationship shaken
strained but not broken.

You worked same company
more than thirty years.
I came and went
lived and worked
seven states
five countries
many exits and entries
a sort of life
inexplicable
as your life
the way lives are
as we try to learn
who we are

all the ares we are
struggle with doubt
fear and failure
profit and loss
to believe in something
to stand for something
to die knowing something
knowing (in the end) how little
we know. Across states
countries and continents
we were in touch via postcards
letters cassettes telephone Skype
mutual love of jazz and standards
keeping us connected.

In your nineties life winding
down dementia eroding
memory erasing a lifetime
of connections I completed
your sentences anticipated
your thoughts gradually losing
you to nods and smiles
as you slipped into silence.

Pushing your wheelchair outside
assisted living the last time
around us nature swelled
I covered you with a blanket
though it was high summer

your mottled hands gripped
the armrests your bones sharp
and skeletal. In shade we sat
by the pond gazing at geese
and piles of white clouds
impossibly big in the sky
blue as your eyes. I took
our photo with my phone
and sent it to my kids —
your grandkids — they sent back
photos from respective locales
and then a video of you waving
and they waved back in theirs
before I wheeled you back
to your room.

Arriving Section Q2
Lot 44 Grave 5
journey's end
here to rest
next to Charlotte
you are lucky
the weather fine today
a good day (you would say)
for golf not gray
no rain spitting
no dead leaves rattling
in cold wind
as on the November day

eight years gone when
she was buried here.

Taking leave
before your ashes
are lowered
I recall the day
not so long ago
your hands bracketing
as I wobbled
on awkward red bike
that weighed a ton
the way you let go
and I rode off
first time
no training wheels away
from your open arms
forever.

MIND'S EYE VIEW

• TO A THAI CONSTRUCTION WORKER •

Your shovel shake gravel grate wakes me
in the flip-flop morning: break new ground
before the break of day. Wheelbarrow turning,
makes the world go round. In denim shirt,
striped *phaasin*, straw hat, and dark scarf
(masking your face like a bandit) you cart
stone, shoulder steel on sunbaked Bangkok *soi*.
At grinding noon, sweat stains your dusty denim
deeper shades of blue. From bamboo scaffold
your eyes tender a greeting. The boundaries
of your universe bump the boundless frontiers
of my imagination. No need to speak. Talk
and labor both are cheap.

· WHERE YOU BELONG ·

You know the place at once: late-afternoon
light slants sharply through the window,
illuminating fragrant frangipani floating
in the embossed silver water bowl placed
on the table reserved just for you.
A delicate breeze strokes a glass-bead curtain,
dancing light prisms splash sky-blue walls.
A haunting *molam* is playing, which you recall
hearing once, half-asleep, traveling by bus
through Isaan, the words inscrutable, save
for the plaintive singer's echoing allusions
to Chaiyaphum. The server knows exactly
what you want. After serving a perfect plate
of *khao niaw ma-muang*, he offers the best cup
of coffee you've ever had. As evening falls,
a *tukkae* calls nine times. An auspicious number,
so you've been told.

· LOST IN TRANSLATION (A Latin Romance) ·

No Se Permiten Escenas Amorosas.
—sign in Vaca Muca Restaurante, La Fortuna, Costa Rica

No love scenes permitted.
This is a family establishment.
Proper decorum is required at all times.
We expect all patrons to be on their best behavior.
You have no license to be licentious under this roof.
Permissiveness is not permitted on these premises.
Prurient interest is not in our interest —
or yours.

It goes without saying:
No balcony scenes,
moonlight serenades,
cloaks in the mud;
Not to mention
rending clothing,
ripping bodice,
crooning,
spooning,
or swooning.

We run a tight ship.
Loose lips
and hips
sink ships.
Don't rock the boat.

This is not an erogenous zone.
Extinguish all love lights.
Check your hormones at the door.
The congregation of two or more persons
for purposes of amorous intent
constitutes unlawful assembly
and is viewed with utmost contempt.
Pas de deux and *ménage à trios* are untenable,
and violate our zero-tolerance policy,
which is nonnegotiable.

All lust abandon, ye who enter here.
This is not the place to start or carry on
an affair. Popping the question is out
of the question. Indecent, provocative,
or revealing attire will provoke our ire,
and is just cause for prompt eviction.

Discretion is the better part of indiscretion.
Entertaining impure thoughts involving
restaurant staff or fellow patrons is
unthinkable; don't even think about it. (If you
think we don't know what you're thinking,
think again.)

Patrons will kindly refrain from making eyes
over plates of rice and beans and plantains.
Suggestive smiles are frowned upon.
We won't hear of sighing, moaning, or
audible breathing of any kind, intensity, or

duration. Pleas of temporary insanity will all
fall upon deaf ears.

This restaurant is a grope-free zone.
Keep your hands to yourself. Hanky-panky
above or below the table is not encouraged.
Caressing or fondling body parts is
beyond the pale and will result
in immediate expulsion,
without fail.

Breaches of etiquette, including (but not
restricted to) Freudian slips, or momentary
lapses of reason, good judgment and taste,
will not be tolerated or excused.
Amour fou will never do.
This means you.

Management reserves the right to refuse
service to anyone conducting him/her
self in a crude, lewd, or otherwise dis-
respectful manner.
Mind your manners.

This sign is not here for decoration.
Your understanding and kind cooperation
is appreciated.

· ATHENS PERSONAL ·

Seeking caryatid for restoration project on Acropolis.
Immediate start. This high-profile post could lead
to permanent position for right candidate. Excellent
posture required. Looking for group player, willing
to pull own weight and exhibit grace under pressure.
Previous heavy lifting in classical environs desirable.
Must love working outdoors with ongoing exposure
to the elements. Ability to handle heavy workload
under intense public scrutiny essential. Exclusive
period clothing provided. We offer a supportive
working environment in spectacular ancient setting.
Apply in person. No email or phone calls, please.

· APRIL FOOL ·

There's a spot on your tie.
Your shoelace is untied.
Believe you forgot to zip
up your fly. The copier just ate
your report that was late;
the file wasn't saved,
chalk one up to fate.
An insidious virus is attacking
your software as we speak;
tech support is unavailable
until next week. I forwarded
the incriminating email
you shared in confidence
to the entire company.
Totally careless, I shouldn't
have done; nevertheless,
it was kind of fun.
Don't look now: your outbox
is in, and your inbox is out.
You've got mail — slap-dash
doggerel, mindless verse.
Don't take it too hard,
things could always be
worse.

· IN YOUR DREAM NOIR ·

for Richard Hugo

You are in the apartment waiting for the others,
a hefty bundle alongside you on the couch wrapped
in newspaper bound with twine. You're dying
to untie it but curiosity killed the cat,
and the Fat Man will open it. If he shows.

You shouldn't have had a drink. The whiskey
was tantalizing in the cut-glass decanter
on the silver tray and coffee table. Your head
is wooly, the room stuffy. You may have slipped
yourself an inadvertent mickey. You try to stand,
but your legs have gone rubber. You graze
the coffee table, taking the decanter with you
on the way down . . ..

The room reemerges, slightly out of kilter . . .
The door bursts open, revealing
Humphrey B. in *Casablanca* trench coat and fedora;
Eddie G. sober in pinstriped three piece;
Jimmy C. in dapper dove-gray double breasted.

Cagney struts in and does a George M. Cohan pirouette,
a Yankee doodle dandy. Bogart and Robinson follow,
sans dance moves. You feel like a patient
in an operating room flat out on a gurney, facing
a team of suspect surgeons.

Cagney wears an impish smirk. Bogart sucks
the ubiquitous coffin nail. Robinson is fretful, channeling
Barton Keyes in *Double Indemnity*.

Cagney picks up the decanter, sniffs disapprovingly. *A shame
to waste good whiskey.*

Bogart blows a cloud of smoke in assent.

You struggle to right yourself and manage to slouch
onto the couch. Finding your voice, you mumble,
Where's the Fat Man? And what about Cairo?

Bogie gives you the stink eye. *You ask too many questions.*

We were going to ask you the same, Robinson adds,
his restless eyes rummaging the room.

Cagney paces the room, walking on the balls
of his feet like a boxer. *It doesn't add up,* he says,
fingering wide lapels. *But then math was never
my strong suit.*

The telephone rings. You trade pointed glances.

Answer it, Robinson barks.

You reach for the phone . . .

It's your alarm clock.

Alcohol and smoke-soaked visions linger.
The stuff dreams are made of.

· DOGS IN THE WINDOW ·

Doggie day care, a mom tells her young son, pausing
at the Chelsea storefront window with the red awning
and white bone logo to watch the dog assembly inside,
before moving on. I dither to revel in canine clientele,
a daily routine on my way to work. Lately, I've taken
to naming the regulars: there's Willie the whippet, lean
and nimble; Bert the beagle, stoic in hound melancholy;
the elegant Italian greyhounds, Federico and Giulietta;
the wieners, Max and Lili (*We're dachshunds!* I hear
their barking protest in my mind's ear); and cool Raoul,
urbane French poodle.

Newly abandoned, the dogs present a picture of angst. One
or two — unflappable, resigned to routine — hunker down
for a nap. A few stalwart rebels scale steps to the windowsill,
their searching eyes begging the universal question,
Why am I here?

Come evening, the dogs are all anticipation. Jumpy, twitchy,
they fidget and pace, some bouncing about like pogo sticks,
collective attention fixed on the door through which owners
will pass, all in good dog time.

On the way home I dally once more, bidding fond farewell:

Good night, sleek Willie.
Good night, blue Bert.
Ciao, Federico, Giulietta.
Wiedersehen, Max und Dear Lili.
Au revoir, Raoul, et bonne chance.
Good night, fine gentlemen,
sweet ladies, good night.

· THE WAVE ·

The animated Gumby clock is not there.
I pass the children's shop on the way to work
each morning and, unfailingly, it's there
in the window: green plastic Gumby smiling,
standing tall, cocked right arm waving,
clock belly rotund as a happy Buddha,
left arm cradling clock as if it might roll off,
two sturdy legs, thick as tree trunks, rooted
to the floor.

Not today.

Gone.

Godzilla's there, sure, but there's menace enough
in the city, no call for lunging dinosaur — teeth bared,
claws splayed, frozen in Frankenstein walk, absent
humor and grace.

Someone must have bought the clock, failing
to consider the fallout, calculate the ripple effect
on casual passersby going about business
their daily way, who counted on that salute,
the Gumby greeting, to make their day.

· FORTUNE COOKIE ·

The rubber bands are heading in the right direction.
—from Mr. Wok & Sushi, Tenafly, New Jersey

This is news. And it starts you wondering
about the rubber bands: where they're from,
where exactly they might be going, what this
could possibly mean — the implications
for life as you know it.

Sounds, first blush, like a good thing; you wouldn't
want the rubber bands going in the wrong direction.
That said, the notion of rubber bands heading
any direction, apparently of their own volition,
is disconcerting. Suppose, for example, they were
covert weapons with the aim, particularly heading
in the right direction, of inflicting damage or pain.
On the other hand, why ascribe nefarious intent?

It would be a mistake to take this personally.
The, not *Your*, rubber bands are at issue here.
To assume that they (whatever they are) have anything
to do with you (wherever they may be heading)
would be paranoid by any stretch of the imagination.

You are overthinking this. It's a fortune cookie.
A culinary postscript. Take a deep breath.

Perhaps it's enough that (somewhere) the rubber bands
moving through this (or parallel) universe — are heading

in the right direction; that, in best-case scenario,
your ducks are in a row, the planets aligned,
the universe unfolding as it should.

Look on the bright side.
Take a walk in the sun.
Count your blessings.

Imagine if your fortune read, *The killer spring rolls are headed*
in your specific direction.

You'd have to leave town fast. No forwarding address.
And Mr. Wok would get no more of your business.

· AN OX GONE MISSING ·

after the painting by Lee Ku-Mo

Hat on, head bowed, shoulders slumped, bamboo switch
tucked under arm, back bent, barefoot, you stand bemused
before broken trail of ox tracks, scattered like coffee beans,
black and brown, a quizzical look on your face
as if to say, *But it was here a moment ago* . . .

You scrutinize the winding track of hoof prints
as if it was an encrypted message, which, were you
to crack the code, might reveal perhaps a path
to enlightenment; failing that, the whereabouts
of your wayward beast. It is not so easy
after all to misplace an ox — not, say, like losing
the car keys or your place in a book.

And yet, weighing this void that once was ox —
a blank slate, excepting said smattering of tracks
and blood-smudged sun on empty sky — perhaps it is
not so strange to have an ox gone missing.
Lives have holes, gaping and empty, more than
sufficient for an ox to pass through.

· DACHSHUND DREAMING ·
—for Chico

Our old dachshund is dreaming, twitching
and yelping on the bedroom floor. Might
this be payback for rabbits he has killed
mercilessly, years past, in the backyard,
running them down before they could escape
under the fence, slamming them down dead,
presenting proudly limp bodies for inspection?
Ghost rabbits may be hounding him now, flitting
about the yard, vanishing whenever he snaps
his jaws going for the jugular. Or, perhaps he is
trapped in some night-of-the-hopping-dead
scenario: legions of grisly zombie rabbits are
stalking him, flesh torn, entrails dangling,
dripping copious trails of blood.

Then again, maybe he's being tormented by
all the squirrels he has pissed off, now avenging
their close encounters with his fangs. Not content
to taunt him with derisive chatter in trees just
out of reach, they're launching a fusillade
of acorns, sugar-gum spike balls, pine cones,
and other arboreal materiel.

But what do I know?

He might be having the time of his life — running endless, open fields, eating his fill of grass he will later vomit, rolling with pure pleasure and impunity in patches of noisome, unspeakable filth.

· THE MEETING ·

Bullet points flying, graphics run amok — we were told
to double down, seize the window of opportunity, go for
the low-hanging fruit. To ensure we had enough skin
in the game (not to put too fine a point on it), they told us
to be proactive out of the box, hit the ground running.
Our numbers in the toilet and headed south, we had
to take a deep dive, drill down, take it to the next level.
The time for spit-balling was past, they said, no more
throwing spaghetti at the wall. To cut to the chase
(and not get lost in the weeds), going forward it was
all about synergy. This was a game changer. We had
to be on point, get on the same page, think outside
the box — push the envelope, move the needle — to stay
ahead of the curve, anticipate the next paradigm shift.

Would there be pushback?

Sure, they conceded. We would have to manage expectations.

Synergy, my ass, someone was heard to mutter
in the pause that followed.

To be sure, we had our doubts. Our plates were full.
Increasing bandwidth by adding projects not
in our wheelhouse seemed a zero-sum game. We were
having trouble getting our heads around it.
That being said, we were reluctant to open up a can
of worms on our watch.

So, when they looped back to propose (as action points)
that we connect the dots, we thought,
Well, it is what it is.

At the end of the day, all things being equal,
we were left wondering whether there was
really a there there.

STRANGE BEAUTY OF THE WORLD

I cannot believe that the inscrutable universe turns on an axis of suffering; surely the strange beauty of the world must somewhere rest on pure joy!

—Louise Bogan, "Little Lobelia"

· A GIFT SUPREME ·

I want to be the force which is truly for good.
—John Coltrane, in a 1966 radio interview

Holding the album first time: feel the gravitas. Spreading
the gatefold — behold: his dual profile, in black & white,
front & back, looking serious as your life. Liner notes
on the facing sides — first surprise: DEAR LISTENER.

Speaking to *you*.

Reading his words, expressing humility, gratitude, praise;
above all, a revelation, a spiritual awakening: losing
the way mid-life, in a dark place, finding that all paths lead
to God.

And so the music, his four-part suite.

The needle drops: inaugural gong, augury of astonishment
to come. His tenor flutters gently, buoyed by thrum
and pulse of bass, piano, and drums. The quartet launches —
slipping bounds of gravity, sun ship outward bound.

As ACKNOWLEDGMENT ends, he chants:

a love supreme
a love supreme
a love supreme . . .

A mantra for life.

The suite unfolds:
RESOLUTION. PURSUANCE. PSALM.

His journey, an offering — grateful for the means to reach
out through music, for the privilege of being here.

And he thanks you,
with love,
for listening.

· FULL MOON IN MALACCA ·

New Year's Eve. Full moon. Roaming alone,
adrift in Malaysia, year nearly spent, tonight
you're bent on shooting the moon, ready
to bet the farm on an auspicious beginning —
a fool gladly on a fool's errand.

The moon abides, dwelling in possibility.

Wandering mostly empty streets in search
of a bar, a beer, and whatnot, what you get
is scant good cheer to usher in a new year.
Rats scurry on sidewalks, rustle in drains,
rattle last-ditch rubbish, detritus of year past
strewn along deserted arcades. Along the river,
monitor lizards swish from the embankment,
disperse in dark water. On street corners, knots
of immobile trishaw drivers slump in idle chariots,
asleep at the handlebars. They seem to have
the right idea. A dance club sign declares,
Sorry, Full House. Indifferent doormen wave
you off.

The full-house moon gives nothing away.

The *Malacca Inn* has closed, so too the *Ace Bar*,
your ace in the hole. Across a bridge looms
Texax Fast Food, a clean, well-lighted place.
Too-well lighted you discover upon entering —

a blinding box of florescence. The clientele
are Chinese men; the few women are servers.
From one you order a beer, seeking some shred
of festive atmosphere. You soak up the beer,
exposed in unforgiving light like a gecko fixed
on a wall, feeling full weight of a dying year fall.

In an adjoining room, sealed behind glass
like a vast aquarium, a sort of party is in progress.
A determined Chinese woman is singing,
gesticulating dramatically on stage. The crowd
of mostly Chinese men claps sedately
at selected intervals. A sign in Chinese and English
warns, *Guest Singers Prohibited on the Stage.*
You are reminded this is not Thailand, where
all the world is a stage, all singers are permitted,
everywhere.

You make your exit. No one takes your cue.

On the street, turning a corner: struck dumb-founded
by the moon.

Luminous sphere, harsh mistress,
loneliest night of the year:
shine your light on all who wander,
let all remain in light.

Approaching your hotel, you glimpse a young woman
framed in a second-story window, face shrouded
in shadow, her freshly washed hair, raven black, long

and straight, burnished, bathed in moonlight. To her
you pledge the moment, dedicate the night, proclaim,
by all power vested in you by the moon,

Let a new year begin.

· MĀNOA VALLEY QUARTET ·

i.
A playground sparrow
perches on basketball rim.
Call it goaltending.

ii.
To fashion their nests,
two birds glean strands from a mop.
Ah! Good housekeeping!

iii.
Royal carpets roll
in rush of red hibiscus
across green hedges.

iv.
Carp arcs from green pool.
Passing cloud crosses pale moon.
All is transient.

· SEEING RED ·

A cardinal whistles strings of song. In the yard
my wife and I survey the bare old tree, mottled
with mold, diseased and dying. A sunlight shaft
scores a bull's eye on blood-red head and breast.
We call our daughter to come and see. Slamming
out the side door, she skips along the driveway,
stops, looks up, eyes scanning sky, birdcall falling
like tumbling ball down a stair. Spying the cardinal,
radiant in heart of light, her arms lift: fingers splay,
wriggle, reach for the sky. She leaps, as if to fly,
ride the wind, defy
gravity.

· WATCHING A METEOR SHOWER
   FROM A BACKYARD IN NEW JERSEY ·

We nearly slept through it. A neighbor's child had said
that a meteor shower would be visible from around four
that morning. My daughter and I vowed to catch it.

Waking suddenly, I pull jeans over pajamas, slip on
shoes and coat, out the side door, down porch steps,
through the gate, into the backyard and faint light
of impending daybreak, craning my neck, scanning
starkly bare trees, branches skeletal and eerie.

Seeing one, then another meteor streak overhead, I race
inside to wake her. Fast asleep, she springs awake
the way sleeping dogs do. Rushing out, we stand side
by side, watching in wonder flaring meteors flashing by.

What are they?

*They're like pieces of stars that break off and fly
through the sky.*

Do they fall down?

*Some do. Others burn up. Some orbit like planets
or asteroids or stars, so that they pass by Earth
every so often.*

How small we are, words failing,
standing in predawn chill,
witness to such strange beauty,
lost in streaming light
and stardust.

· IN THE MOUNTAINS ABOVE CUSCO ·

Night train strains,
judders jagged way
down steep decline
mountain spine,
back-end day trip
to Machu Picchu,
headlight a blinding
Cyclops eye probing
indigo sky.
In distant valley
Cusco appears —
Plaza de Armas
awash
in wondrous white:
a basket of light.

· MIRAFLORES NOCTURNE ·

Precipitous cliffs, caressed by crescent bay, curl
like a sleeping cat, defining the coast of Lima.

A steady lighthouse beam sweeps the night,
demarcating the arc of unknown.

Across the bay, a luminous cross stands,
steadfast sentinel ministering to the night.

Bracketing the bay, the dual beacons beckon,
staking their respective claims.

Along the cliff top, the Parque del Amor lounges
in shadow and moonlight.

· NIGHT FALLS IN THE PARQUE DEL AMOR ·

Couples cluster
on benches
snuggle
by boulders
on paths meandering
along cliffs skirting
the half-moon bay —
erogenous array
in the park of love.

Bodies entwine
cling like brush binding
fragile rock face
alone together
coast of Miraflores,
Lima, Peru,
edge of known world
in suspended night.

Concupiscent moon
overflows on the bay.
A young girl sells candy
along the way,
moonlight reflects
in her silver tray.

· UNDER YOUR NOSE ·

Advertising an appliance superstore, the billboard boasted:
The best prices in town are right under your nose.

Jutting from the sign, an enormous nose,
made of who knew what, sticking out surreally
like a sore thumb. Super schnozzle! Proboscis colossus!
Brash and flashy, you couldn't miss it, plain as the nose
on your face — in your face, tasteless as it was delightful.
Marcel Duchamp would have approved, a masterpiece
of neo-Dada, fin-de-twentieth-siècle art.

For months the sign looked down its nose
at we NJ commuters on daily pilgrimage,
by bus and car, to and from Gotham. Oddly affecting,
it cast an eccentric magic; to fall under its spell was
to anticipate the daily sightings, insistent and predictable
as the Manhattan skyline.

All things must pass. One gray winter day it happened:
a team of billboard surgeons had amputated the nose,
their gargantuan crane parked roadside like a frozen dinosaur,
the severed nose abandoned on the ground, a ridge
of crusty snow coating its massive bridge,
as morning traffic roared past.

Going home that night, passing the mutilated sign
on the highway, the nose was gone.

In the ensuing void a question lingers: *Whither the nose?*

Destined for landfill?

Scrapped as junk?

Warehoused in limbo,
where curious objects
made redundant repose,
pending reincarnation?

Idle speculation.

Where the nose goes,
the nose only knows.

· MANHATTAN EVENFALL ·

Crimson tulips
row on row
buds clenched
in bloody fists
erect soldiers
stand at attention
awaiting orders
to bloom.

Chrysler Building
Deco crown
magic moment
sparked
by twilight
radiant arcs
revealing jewels
of light.

• FROST VARIATIONS •

i.

Rime dusts the dead leaves, fragile
as moth wings. White crystals shimmer
in morning light.

ii.

Hedgerow glazed in shaved ice,
snowsheet spread on evergreen bed —
frosting on the cake.

iii.

Baldhead half-dome trashcan hooded
in ice; the lid, sunny side,
sweating bullets.

· SPRING MANIFESTATIONS ·

The backyard is teeming
with robins. Orange breasts
spring and ripple, flapping
about sprouting green lawn
like prayer flags.

Holding down the perimeter,
a handful of squirrels cavort
among nascent crocus shoots.

· WINTER ORPHAN ·

From icy sidewalk
a homeless glove reaches out.
No one lends a hand.

· SNOWY NIGHT, DRIVING HOME ·

Crossing incessant span of Tappan Zee Bridge
at length exiting madhouse Route 287
onto 9W South somewhere Zen New Jersey;
outside, snow whirling, wipers slapping,
headlights sucking snowflakes
like hungry vacuum cleaners.

Inside, mix tape playing:
Andy Summers' *Rainforest in Manhattan*
segues to
Carlos Santana's *Samba de Sausalito*,
and then
Oceanic Beloved, Alice Coltrane's
angelic harp.

Thinking how most people would
not want to be caught dead driving
on a night like this; for me, it's perfect:
I'm alive, and I could sail
snow-blown streets
riding rivers of music
drifting in black
and white
forever.

· I WAS FLYING ·

I was flying
in vast expanse
of starry night
and snowy peaks
(the Himalaya,
so I imagined)
soaring
in wondrous cold
thrilled
chilled
in such rare
atmosphere
suddenly
descending
and then crashing
feet first
through double doors
of an old wooden library
sliding
across the dusty floor
(as into home plate)
people at tables inside
looking up
a moment
and then back
to their reading

as if I were
some rowdy patron
returning
an overdue book.

· BLUE UMBRELLA ·

Like an alien spacecraft
the blue umbrella hovers
above the woman in red
moving in twilight mist
on rain-slicked sidewalk
through the French Concession.
Her insistent gait makes
no concession;
red dress gives
no quarter. Staring
into that fire is to stare
at the sun; surrendering
to blindness demands
headlong flight
to flame.
Blue umbrella passes.
Red glow fizzles,
an ember dying
in Shanghai drizzle.
Temperature
drops.
Breath returns.
Go ahead, now.
Breathe.

· RAOUL DUFY ·

One must meditate about pleasure. Raoul Dufy is pleasure.
—Gertrude Stein

Born in Le Harve to a large family,
first child of nine was Raoul Dufy.

Receiving a grant at age twenty-three,
studied painting in fin-de-siècle Paris.

Matisse and the Fauves helped him free
his color and line from mimicry.

With my eyes and my heart I paint what I see.
Nature was just a theory to Raoul Dufy.

Bright colors, broad brushstrokes spontaneously
such were the hallmarks of Raoul Dufy.

The thing itself does not interest me;
it's the way it's presented, said Raoul Dufy.

Parades, horse races, pleasure boats on the sea,
sport and leisure were the province of Raoul Dufy.

No one painted the sky, no one painted the sea
in such marvelous blues as Raoul Dufy.

His eyes erased all he considered ugly;
never painted a sad picture, did Raoul Dufy.

· IT WAS ALL ABOUT BEAUTY (Song for Charlie) ·

It's important for bass players to enhance everything behind
the solos in order to inspire the musicians to play better than
they've ever played before. That's what I try to do.
—Charlie Haden, in a radio interview on *Fresh Air*

Yours was a deep
beautiful music
never a question of
country
folk
bebop
free jazz
gospel
blues
for you (like Duke Ellington)
it was just music
beyond category
everything you played
with open ears
and open heart
nothing superfluous
less was more
each note
a personal journey
an affirmation of life
and human spirit
it was all about beauty
every vibration
a foil for sadness

and ugliness
a rebellion against
the meanness
violence and injustice
in the world
restless rambling boy
bringing joy
when you lifted
your bass you lifted
everyone up.

· ON FINISHING *THE LITTLE PRINCE* ·

"Were they not satisfied where they were?" asked the little
prince.
"No one is ever satisfied where he is," said the switchman.
—Antoine de Saint-Exupéry, *The Little Prince*

St.-Ex, exile in New York City, lost, longing
for home, for wind, sand, and stars, there was
a kind of salvation in your little prince: a state
of grace, fleeting reprieve from final smash up.
When you drew the two lines crossing, spare
and elegant as calligraphy, and one star suspended
above the loveliest, saddest landscape in the world,
perhaps in that moment you grasped, having flown
often with death to die another day, that your luck
would run out, that one day, like Icarus, you must fall
to embrace the welcoming sea; and, having seen
rightly with your heart, it would all be worth it.

· BENEDICTION ·

No matter what one believes in, there is something wonderful about blessing things.
—Kathleen Norris, *Dakota*

A single blackbird rests
on arm of gold-leaf cross
atop gold-leaf dome
on pale-green bell tower
above concrete church
with red roof tiles; lone sentry,
as night comes on. A mass
of purple clouds coalesces
in dying light. The blackbird
trills a blessing, and then takes
flight.

NOTES

WAITING FOR THE BIG ONE   15
Years after the U.S. dropped an atomic bomb on Nagasaki, Japanese photographer Shomei Tomatsu photographed the remains of a wristwatch dug up near the explosion. The watch had stopped at 11:02 a.m on August 9, 1945, the exact moment the bomb fell.

Dick and Jane were fictional characters in basal reading texts widely used in U.S. elementary schools, particularly in the 1940s and '50s.

TRESPASS   57
Ban Vinai camp was located in Loei province, Thailand. Refugees there were mainly highland Lao, especially Hmong, who had fled the communist Pathet Lao.

A *phaasin* is a long piece of cotton cloth worn as a wraparound by women.

A FITTING GESTURE   58
Nong Khai camp, in Nong Khai province, Thailand, processed Lao and Hmong refugees for third-country resettlement following the fall of Laos to the communist Pathet Lao in 1975.

Q&A   59
Phanat Nikhom camp, established in Chonburi province, Thailand, in July 1980, was initially a processing center for Cambodian refugees escaping the Khmer Rouge. Vietnamese and Laotian refugees were later sent there from other camps to be processed for third-country resettlement.

Following their takeover on April 30, 1975, the communist Khmer Rouge initiated the destruction of all existing political, economic, educational, religious, and cultural institutions in Cambodia. They referred to this revolutionary start over as Year Zero.

The Angkar (the Organization) was the leadership of the Khmer Rouge.

HELPING HAND 60

Galang is a small island in the Riau Archipelago of Indonesia. Galang camp accommodated Vietnamese and Cambodian refugees from 1979 to 1996. An estimated 250,000 refugees passed through Galang during this period. Most were Vietnamese.

CAMBODIAN MUSICIANS AND DANCERS PERFORM ON CHRISTMAS NIGHT 63

The Tonle Sap River connects the Tonle Sap Lake in Cambodia to the Mekong River. Annual monsoon rains typically pour so much water into the Mekong River that it briefly forces the Tonle Sap River to flow backwards, increasing the Tonle Sap Lake to more than five times its normal size.

The Bayon is a temple in the ancient city of Angkor Thom, near Siem Reap, Cambodia.

METAMORPHOSIS 66

The Khmer Rouge slogan "To keep you is no benefit; to destroy you is no loss" is quoted by Teeda Butt Mam in her story "Worms from Our Skin," from *Children of Cambodia's Killing Fields: Memoirs of Survivors*, compiled by Dith Pran. 1977, Yale University.

THE MUSEUM OF WAR IS KIND 70

Larry Burrows, Robert Capa, Dickey Chapelle, Henri Huet, Kent Potter, and Keisaburo Shimamoto were photojournalists killed while reporting in various areas of conflict surrounding the French and later American war in Vietnam.

SONG 78

During World War II, some allied soldiers collected paper money, including U.S. dollar bills and low-denomination foreign banknotes, from various countries in which they served. They taped the bills together to make a keepsake known as a "short snorter."

TO A THAI CONSTRUCTION WORKER 91

A *soi* is a side street or lane, branching off a main road.

Molam is a traditional folk music popular in Laos and in Isaan, the northeastern part of Thailand.

Chaiyaphum is the name of a province and its provincial capital in northeastern Thailand.

A *tukkae* is a type of gecko common to Southeast Asia, so named for the call it makes.

ACKNOWLEDGMENTS

A shout out to former colleagues in refugee resettlement and education programs: the Joint Voluntary Agency in Bangkok, Thailand; the Refugee Employment Program in Honolulu, Hawai'i; the Consortium (U.S. Department of State, Save the Children, and Experiment in International Living) in Galang, Indonesia; and Catholic Charities, Diocese of Stockton, California. I learned much from your professionalism, dedication, and compassion.

My thanks to *The Journal: A Publication for English as a Second Language and Cultural Orientation Teachers*, in which previous versions of "Taking Leave" and "Cambodian Musicians and Dancers Perform on Christmas Night" first appeared.

I gratefully acknowledge Seth Mydans, the former Southeast Asia Bureau Chief for *The New York Times*, for his consistently insightful reporting, particularly on Cambodia following the Khmer Rouge genocide. His articles helped inform "Metamorphosis" and "To Destroy Evil."

My very special thanks to Pamela Hartmann, for her many insightful comments and suggestions.

I am indebted to Marian Haley Beil for her expertise in editing and designing this book.

And always, my gratitude and love to Mintari, Jason, and Jessica.

Bill Preston was a community organizer in a VISTA project in Yonkers, New York. He later taught at-risk students at an alternative school there. In the Peace Corps, he taught English and trained Thai teachers of English; subsequently, he interviewed Lao and Khmer  refugees seeking asylum in the Unites States. At Galang camp, he trained Indonesian teachers, who taught English to Vietnamese refugees. For many years he edited English Language Teaching materials for several educational publishers. As a member of the NYC Civic Corps, he engaged public school students in community service projects.

www.ingramcontent.com/pod-product-compliance
Lightning Source LLC
Chambersburg PA
CBHW020658260626
47157CB00008B/3087